Arthur's Camp-Out

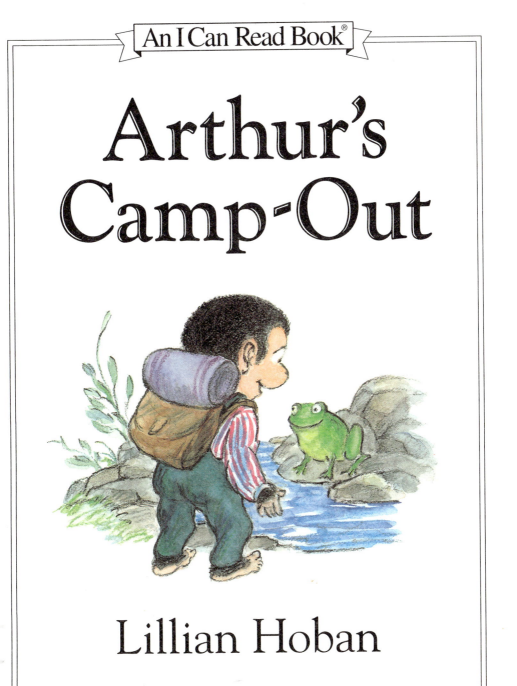

Lillian Hoban

■ HarperCollins*Publishers*

For Elias

HarperCollins®, ☕®, and I Can Read Book®
are trademarks of HarperCollins Publishers Inc.

Arthur's Camp-Out
Copyright © 1993 by Lillian Hoban
Printed in the U.S.A. All rights reserved.

Library of Congress Cataloging-in-Publication Data
Hoban, Lillian.
    Arthur's camp-out / Lillian Hoban.
      p.   cm. — (An I can read book)
    Summary: Bored with spring vacation, Arthur decides to go
alone on a overnight field trip in the woods behind his house.
    ISBN 0-06-020525-3. — ISBN 0-06-020526-1 (lib. bdg.)
    [1. Camping—Fiction. 2. Chimpanzees—Fiction.] I. Title.
II. Series.
PZ7.H635Aq   1993   91-27528
[E]—dc20   CIP
                                                   AC

5 6 7 8 9 10
❖

Chapter
1

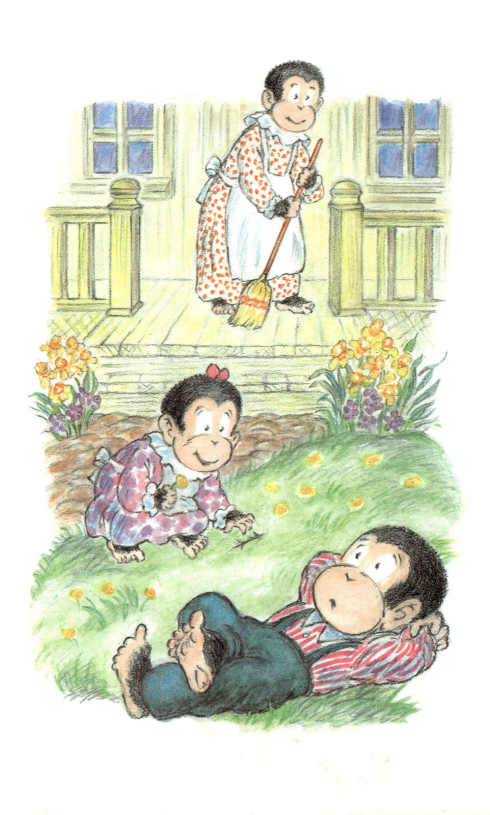

It was spring vacation.

Mother and Father were away.

The baby-sitter was

sweeping the porch.

Violet was in the yard

picking dandelions.

Arthur was lying on the grass.

"Come look at this bug,"

said Violet.

"It looks like a twig."

"It's a walkingstick," said Arthur.

"We studied them in science."

Arthur yawned and rolled over.

"I wish I had something to do."

"I will tell you what you can do,"

called the baby-sitter.

"You can clean up the yard."

"That's *nothing* to do,"

said Arthur.

"Yes, it is," said the baby-sitter.

"You can pick up

all the broken branches and twigs."

"But not my walkingstick twig,"
said Violet.

"He will not know the difference,"
said Arthur.

"He might," said Violet.

8

"No, he won't,"

said Arthur.

"You never studied science.

So you don't know."

"Yes, I did," said Violet.

"My teacher put some cocoons

in glass jars.

After a while, moths came out."

"That's baby science,"

said Arthur.

"I mean real science,

like going on field trips

and collecting specimens."

"How about collecting

some trash specimens,"

said the baby-sitter.

She gave Arthur a big trash bag.

"Phooey," said Arthur.

"Why can't I do
something fun?"

Arthur started to clean up the yard.

He picked up branches and twigs.

He picked up an old gum wrapper.

He picked up a Cracker Jack box.

Inside the box was a big black ant.

It was carrying

a piece of Cracker Jack.

"Look, Violet," said Arthur.

"Here is a worker ant—

just like we studied in science."

Violet looked at the ant.

"I thought you studied specimens,"
she said.

"An ant is a specimen," said Arthur.
"Our class goes on field trips
to collect them.

Oh boy! I just got a great idea.

I *am* going to do something fun.

I'm going to go on a field trip."

"Can I come too?"

asked Violet.

"No," said Arthur.

"I want to collect frogs

and worms and snakes—

slimy things that

you would not like."

"A girl in my class brought in

a snake she caught," said Violet.

"It wasn't a bit slimy.

I held it in my hand."

"You did?" asked Arthur.

"Yes," said Violet.

"Okay," said Arthur.

"You can come on the field trip.

Go get some glass jars with lids."

Chapter 2

Wilma and her big sister, Mabel,

came down the road.

They had knapsacks and blanket rolls

on their backs.

Wilma's knapsack had

pots and pans tied to it.

Mabel's knapsack had

water jugs tied to it.

"Where are you going

with all that stuff?"

asked Arthur.

"We're going on a camp-out,"

said Wilma.

"We came to ask Violet
to come with us," said Mabel.
"Violet is going on a field trip
with me," said Arthur.

"When I was young, I used to go
on field trips," said Mabel.
"They are okay,
but camping out is more fun."

Just then Violet came out

with the glass jars.

"We're going on a camp-out

in the woods behind your house,"

said Mabel.

"We're going to build a fire

and cook hot dogs

and toast marshmallows

and tell ghost stories

and sing songs.

Do you want to come?"

"Can Arthur come too?" asked Violet.

"Arthur is going on a field trip,"

said Mabel.

"Aren't you, Arthur?"

"Oh, I don't know," said Arthur.

"Maybe I should go on your camp-out.

Then I could protect you

in the woods at night."

"Huh!" said Mabel.

"I'm in charge of this camp-out.

I don't need anyone to protect me!

You're not even old enough to build a

campfire.

Come on, Violet.

Go get your knapsack

and a blanket roll.

We will have lots of fun

without Arthur!"

"Who wants to go on a camp-out
with a bunch of girls?" said Arthur.
"I'm going on a field trip
to collect specimens.
And maybe I will camp out overnight
all by myself!"

Chapter
3

Arthur packed his pajamas
and his toothbrush.
He packed glass jars for specimens.
Then he went to the kitchen for food.
"My goodness," said the baby-sitter.
"The woods behind the house
will be full of campers tonight!
Here are two peanut-butter and jelly
sandwiches, a banana, an orange,
and a thermos of milk," she said.
"Come home if you get lonely."
"I'm not afraid of being alone
in the woods," said Arthur.

Arthur went out to the yard.

He climbed over the stone wall

and followed the path into the woods.

After a while he came to a brook.

Kerplash!

A frog jumped into the brook.

"Oh boy! My first specimen,"

said Arthur.

The frog hopped onto a stone.

Arthur hopped after the frog.

The stone was slippery

and Arthur slipped *splash*!

right into the water.

The frog hopped away.

"Phooey," said Arthur.

He climbed out of the brook.

His clothes were wet,

his knapsack was wet,

and his blanket roll was wet.

It was getting dark, and he tripped

over the roots of a tree.

"I wish I had a flashlight,"

said Arthur.

Then he saw a little glimmer,

and another, and another.

"Lightning bugs!" cried Arthur.

"I will use them for light!"

He took out his glass jar

and tried to catch one.

It flew into a briar bush.

Arthur dove in after it.

Thorns tore his clothes,

and prickers pricked his fingers.

"Yow!" yelled Arthur,

and he dropped the jar.

He dug around under the bush

till he felt something

round and smooth.

"I found it!" cried Arthur,

and he pulled it up.

Hissssss!

"A SNAKE!" yelled Arthur.

He dropped the snake and ran.

Low-hanging branches

slapped at Arthur's face.

Vines tangled in the straps

of his knapsack.

Arthur pulled off his knapsack.

He held it in front of his face

so he could run faster.

Suddenly he heard *whoosh!*

"Who's there?" called Arthur.

Something swooped
low over his head.

Something zoomed
past his nose.

Then something
squeak, squeaked
near his ear.

43

"BATS!" yelled Arthur.

He dropped his knapsack

and ran as fast as he could.

44

Chapter
4

After a while Arthur stopped

to catch his breath.

It was very quiet.

A pond shimmered in the moonlight.

Arthur sat down

at the edge of the pond.

He was tired,

he was wet,

and he was hungry.

"This is a good place to camp,"

said Arthur,

"but now I don't have anything

to camp with.

"I wish I had something to eat,"
he said.

"Maybe if I go to sleep,
I won't know I'm hungry."
Arthur made a little nest
in some dry leaves.

He was just nodding off when

Buzzzzz . . .

A mosquito buzzed near his ear.

Arthur slapped at the mosquito.

Another one bit him on the nose.

Then another mosquito bit his foot,

and another stung his hand.

"It's my wet clothes," said Arthur.

"If I cover myself with leaves,

they will not come after me."

Arthur covered himself with leaves.

Now all the mosquitoes buzzed

around his head.

Arthur tried to drive them off

by twitching his nose.

"Phooey!" yelled Arthur.

He got up and hopped around,

slapping at the mosquitoes.

Suddenly he stopped and sniffed.

"Hot dogs!" said Arthur.

"I smell hot dogs."

Arthur closed his eyes and

sniffed some more.

"Oh, I'm so hungry!"

Arthur's stomach started to grumble.

It grumbled so loudly,

he could hardly hear the singing

that drifted across the pond.

"It's the girls at their camp-out,"

said Arthur.

"Maybe I can sneak up and find

part of a hot dog someone dropped."

Arthur ran around

to the other side of the pond.

Arthur snuck up to the girls.

He crouched down

in the shadows.

The girls were sitting

around the campfire.

They were roasting hot dogs

and singing:

Here comes Mr. Fuzzy Bat

You buzzy insects better scat

Bats fly low

And bats fly high

Flitting through

The nighttime sky . . .

Arthur's stomach grumbled.

"What was that?"

asked Wilma.

Arthur stumbled out of the shadows.

"Bats!" he cried.

"Why are you singing about bats?

A whole bunch of bats

came after me

and tried to bite me

and I lost my knapsack

and all my camping stuff

and I don't have anything to eat

and I'm hungry!"

"My goodness, Arthur,"

said Mabel.

"You do look like something

came after you."

"It could not be bats," said Violet.

"Bats don't hurt you.

Bats are good.

Bats eat insects like mosquitoes,

and they spread pollen

so more flowers will grow."

"How do *you* know?" asked Arthur.

"We learned about them in science,"

said Violet,

and she gave Arthur a hot dog.

Arthur and the girls

toasted marshmallows and sang songs.

Then they went to sleep.

Arthur dreamed about bats—

thin and fat bats,

small and tall bats.

They were all friendly.

In the morning, Arthur said,

"I dreamed about bats.

They told me

where to find my knapsack."

Arthur did find his knapsack.

It was where

the bats said it would be.

When the campers came home,

there was a big sign

over the porch that said:

The baby-sitter

made stacks of pancakes

with lots of syrup for breakfast.

Arthur and Violet

and Wilma and Mabel sat on the porch

under the sign and ate them all up.

JE
H

Hoban, Lillian.

Arthur's camp-out.

$15.89

REQUIRED READING

BAKER & TAYLOR